The Disney Princess Cookbook

The Disney Princess Cookbook

Recipes by
Cynthia Littlefield

Photography by
Joanne Schmaltz

DISNEP PRESS
New York • Los Angeles

Table of Contents

Even though the Disney Princesses come from many different parts of the world—both land and sea—there's something they all have in common: they love to cook! In this book, you'll find fifty yummy recipes from Rapunzel, Ariel, Cinderella, and all your other favorite Princesses. Just turn the pages to discover delicious ideas for breakfast, lunch, and dinner, as well as tasty beverages, snacks, and desserts.

If you've never cooked before, don't worry! The Princesses chose each dish with beginner cooks in mind. Remember that every recipe's difficulty is rated on a five-crown scale: 👑 👑 👑 👑 👑. That way, you can start by making something easy (👑) and work your way up to the more complicated recipes (👑 👑 👑 👑 👑). So grab your apron and get ready to cook up a royal feast!

Before You Begin

Cooking is a lot of fun, but before you get started, there are some important things to remember. Always, always ask a parent for permission. Even young princesses need to check with the queen or king before they use the palace kitchen. If you need to use a stove, oven, blender, or mixer for a recipe, make sure to ask an adult to help you. Here are a few other tips to keep in mind.

- If you have long hair, tie it back. You don't want it to end up in the food or near a hot stove.

- Make sure your clothing isn't loose enough to touch a stovetop burner. If you're wearing long sleeves, push them up to your elbows.

- Put on an apron to keep your outfit from getting stained.

- Wash your hands so they will be clean when you handle the ingredients.

- Take a few minutes to read the whole recipe so that nothing will come as a surprise once you get started.

- Gather all the equipment you'll need, such as measuring spoons, bowls, baking pans, and utensils, before you get out the ingredients.

Measuring Ingredients

To make sure a recipe turns out just the way it's supposed to, you need to measure ingredients exactly. Here are some helpful hints and tips.

- For liquids like milk, water, or vegetable oil, use a measuring cup with a spout designed for pouring.

- A dry ingredient, such as flour, sugar, or cocoa, should be spooned into a measuring cup without a spout. Then, to check that you have the exact amount, scrape the flat edge of a butter knife across the rim of the cup to remove any extra.

- A chunky ingredient should be spooned into a measuring cup and then patted gently, just enough to even out the top without packing it down. Shredded ingredients are also measured this way.

- Brown sugar should be packed into measuring cups to press out any air bubbles.

- Measuring butter is really easy if you use sticks that have tablespoon marks printed on the wrapper. All you have to do is slice the butter where the line is.

Safety First!

A good cook never forgets that safety always comes first in the kitchen. Here are some important rules to follow.

Using knives, peelers, graters, and small kitchen appliances

- Never use a kitchen appliance or sharp utensil without asking an adult for help.

- Always use a cutting board when slicing or chopping ingredients. Grip the knife handle firmly, holding it so that the sharp edge is facing downward. Then slice through the ingredient, moving the knife away from yourself.

- After slicing raw meat or fish, wash the knife (with adult help) as well as the cutting board. You should also wash your hands really well before working with other ingredients.

- If you drop a knife, don't try to catch it. Instead, quickly step back and let the knife fall to the countertop or floor before picking it up by the handle.

- When using a vegetable peeler, press the edge of the blade into the vegetable's skin and then push the peeler away from yourself. Keep in mind that the more pressure you use, the thicker the peeling will be.

- Use electrical appliances, such as mixers and blenders, in a cleared space far away from the sink and other wet areas. And always unplug a mixer or blender before scraping a mixture from the beaters or blades.

Working around hot things

- Always ask an adult for help around a hot stovetop or oven.

- Make sure to point the handle of a stovetop pan away from you so you won't knock into it and accidently tip the pot over.

- Use pot holders every time you touch a stovetop pot or skillet—even if it's just the lid. You should also use pot holders whenever you put a pan in the oven or take it out.

- Remember, steam can burn! Be sure to step back a bit when straining hot foods, such as pasta or cooked vegetables.

- Don't forget to shut off the oven or stove burner when the food is done baking or cooking.

Preparing Fruits and Vegetables

It's important to wash produce before adding it to a recipe. Here are some tips for making sure fruits and vegetables are clean and ready to use.

- Rinse produce well under plain running water. Don't use soap! If the produce is firm, like an apple or carrot, rub the surface to help remove any garden soil or grit. You can put softer fruits and vegetables, such as berries and broccoli florets, in a small colander or strainer before rinsing.

- Use a vegetable brush to scrub vegetables that grow underground, like potatoes and carrots. You should also scrub any fruits and vegetables that grow right on the ground, such as cucumbers and melons.

- Dry washed produce with a paper towel and cut off any bruised parts before using it in a recipe.

Cleaning Up

A good cook always leaves the kitchen as tidy as she found it. This means cleaning all the bowls, pots, pans, and utensils you used to prepare the recipe. Here are some tips for making sure everything is spick-and-span.

- Always ask an adult for help washing knives and appliances with sharp blades, such as a blender or food processor.

- As you cook, try to give each bowl and utensil a quick rinse as soon as you're done with it. That way leftover food or batter won't stick to it before you can wash it with soap and water.

- Put all the ingredients back where they belong so you'll know just where to find them the next time you cook.

- Wipe down your work area—including the countertop and sink—with a damp paper towel.

- Double-check that all the appliances you used are turned off before you leave the kitchen.

- Hang up your apron, or put it in the laundry room if it needs to be washed.

Breakfast

1 egg

¾ cup milk

2 Tbsp canola oil

1 Tbsp maple syrup

1 cup flour

2 tsp baking powder

½ tsp salt

Butter or oil for frying

1 or 2 add-ins from
the list below

Add-In Choices

¼ cup grated apple or pear

½ cup blueberries

¼ cup chocolate chips

1 to 2 Tbsp walnut bits

Tip

After the pancakes
cook for a couple of
minutes, lift an edge
with the spatula so you
can check if bottoms
are done cooking.

Pascal's Pancakes

Serves 4 to 6

It's easy to tell when Rapunzel's chameleon friend has a change of heart: he changes color! Inspired by Pascal, you can change this recipe by adding different ingredients to suit *your* mood.

Directions

1. Crack the egg into a large mixing bowl. Whisk in the milk, canola oil, and maple syrup.

2. In a small bowl, whisk together the flour, baking powder, and salt. Add the flour mixture to the egg mixture and stir just until all the ingredients are wet. The batter should be lumpy.

3. Gently stir in the add-ins of your choice. Don't stir too much, though, or the pancakes will be dense.

4. Ask an adult to help you at the stove. Lightly butter or oil a nonstick frying pan, and then warm it on the stovetop over medium heat for about one minute. Turn the heat down to medium low. Use a ¼-cup measuring cup to pour the batter for each pancake into the pan.

5. When the tops of the pancakes start to bubble, carefully flip the pancakes over with a spatula. Continue cooking them until the undersides are golden brown. Serve with butter and maple syrup.

Scrumptious Scottish Scones

Makes 6

Merida loves waking up to the smell of freshly baked scones. Filled with oats and raisins, these delicious Scottish treats are the perfect breakfast before a fun-filled day of adventuring.

Directions

1. Heat the oven to 400°F.

2. In a large bowl, stir together the flour, rolled oats, baking powder, salt, cinnamon, nutmeg, and brown sugar. With a table knife, cut the butter into small pieces. Use your fingertips to pinch the butter into the flour until the lumps of butter are about the size of peas. Mix in the raisins.

3. In a small bowl, whisk the egg and milk together. Stir the egg mixture into the flour mixture until they are evenly combined. Be careful not to stir too long, or the scones will come out dense and heavy instead of fluffy.

4. Turn the dough onto a floured surface. Rub a little flour on your hands and pat the dough into a ¾-inch-thick circle.

5. Now make the topping. Use a pastry brush to spread a teaspoon of milk on the top of the dough. Sprinkle on the tablespoon of brown sugar and the pinch of rolled oats.

6. Cut the circle into 6 triangular pieces, just like you would cut a pie. Place the pieces slightly apart on an ungreased baking sheet.

7. Ask an adult to help you with the oven. Place the tray in the oven, and bake the scones until they start to turn golden brown (about 8 to 10 minutes).

8. Remove the tray from the oven. Let the scones cool for about 5 minutes before eating.

Ingredients

Dough
1 cup flour
¼ cup rolled oats
2 tsp baking powder
½ tsp salt
¼ tsp cinnamon
¼ tsp nutmeg
3 Tbsp packed brown sugar
4 Tbsp cold butter
½ cup raisins
1 large egg
¼ cup milk

Topping
1 tsp milk
1 Tbsp brown sugar
Pinch of rolled oats

Tip

For an extra-sweet treat, substitute a ½ cup of chocolate chips for the raisins.

2 cups plain granola

¼ cup raw sunflower seeds

¼ cup dried fruits,
such as chopped apricots,
pineapple bits, cranberries,
and/or raisins

¼ cup sliced almonds

Tip

Granola is more
than just a breakfast
cereal. It also tastes
great topped with
yogurt, sprinkled on
ice cream, or even
tossed in a salad.

Good Morning Granola

Serves 4 to 6

Cinderella always makes sure to have plenty of sunflower seeds in her kitchen. That way she can feed her bird friends and still have some left over to use in this tasty breakfast granola.

Directions

1. Stir the granola and sunflower seeds together in a big bowl.

2. Choose the dried fruit you want to add. You can pick one or mix a few together. Add the fruit and almonds to the bowl.

3. Stir the granola until all the ingredients are well mixed. It's ready to eat right away.

Miners' Mini Muffins

Makes 2 dozen

Digging for diamonds is a full day's work. That's why the Seven Dwarfs always fuel up with a good breakfast before heading to the mines. These pint-size muffins are one of their favorites.

Directions

1. Heat the oven to 375°F. Lightly grease the bottom of a 24-cup mini muffin pan.

2. In a small mixing bowl, stir together the flour, brown sugar, baking powder, cinnamon, and salt.

3. In a bigger bowl, whisk together the egg, milk, and melted butter.

4. Stir the flour mixture into the egg mixture just until all the ingredients are wet. Use a rubber spatula to gently mix the blueberries into the batter.

5. Spoon the batter into the prepared pan until the muffin cups are about ⅔ full.

6. Ask an adult to help you at the oven. Place the muffin tray in the oven, and bake for about 12 minutes. You can tell if the muffins are done by sticking a toothpick into the center of one or two. If the toothpick comes out clean, the muffins are ready to take out.

7. Let the baked muffins cool in the pan for 2 or 3 minutes before turning them out on a cooling rack.

Ingredients

1 cup flour

½ cup brown sugar

1 tsp baking powder

¼ tsp cinnamon

¼ tsp salt

1 egg

½ cup milk

2 Tbsp butter, melted

½ cup blueberries

Tip

For regular-size muffins, just use a 12-cup muffin pan. Then check the muffins for doneness after 15 to 18 minutes.

Ingredients

2 large eggs

2 Tbsp milk

Dash of salt

Dash of pepper

⅓ Tbsp butter

2 Tbsp of add-ins from the list below

Add-In Choices

Shredded cheddar cheese

Bacon bits

Diced ham

Diced cooked potatoes

Diced red bell pepper

Tip

For scrambled eggs that are soft and fluffy, whisk the mixture an extra minute or two before pouring it in the pan.

Frying-Pan Eggs

Serves 2

👑 👑

It's no secret that Rapunzel knows how to use her frying pan. Luckily for Flynn, this recipe doesn't involve her smacking him with it!

Directions

1. Crack the eggs into a small mixing bowl. Add the milk, salt, and pepper, and whisk all the ingredients together.

2. Ask an adult to help you at the stove. Melt the butter in a skillet over low heat, then pour in the egg mixture.

3. Sprinkle 2 Tbsp of add-ins on top of the eggs.

4. Use a spatula to push the cooking eggs into the center of the pan, allowing the still-liquid egg to flow in underneath. Repeat until there's no liquid left and the eggs are cooked through (about 3 to 4 minutes).

Abu's Monkey Bread

Serves 8 to 10

Sometimes it takes a little convincing to get Abu to share his bread. With this sweet-and-sticky pull-apart treat, there's plenty for everybody!

Directions

1. Heat the oven to 375°F. Generously grease a nonstick fluted tube pan.

2. In a mixing bowl, stir together the flour, baking powder, and salt. With a table knife, cut the butter into small pieces. Use your fingertips to pinch the butter into the flour mixture until the lumps of butter are about the size of peas. Then stir in the milk.

3. Turn the dough onto a floured surface and knead it for about 5 seconds. Pull off pieces of the dough and shape them into 2½ to 3 dozen golf ball-size pieces.

4. Mix the brown sugar, white sugar, and cinnamon together in a small bowl.

5. One at a time, dip the dough balls into the melted butter, roll them in the sugar mixture, and place them in the prepared pan. Stack the balls on top of one another until the pan is full.

6. Ask an adult to help you at the oven. Bake the monkey bread for 20 to 25 minutes. You can tell if the bread is ready by sticking a toothpick into it. If the toothpick comes out clean, the bread is done baking. Set the bread aside to cool for about 10 minutes.

7. Use a small spatula to gently loosen the bread from the sides of the pan. Now it's time to turn the monkey bread out of the pan. Be sure to ask an adult for help with this step! First place a serving dish face down on top of the fluted tube pan. Next, hold the dish and pan together securely, and flip them over. Slowly lift the pan off the plate and release the monkey bread.

8. Let the bread cool slightly. Then pull pieces from it, and enjoy!

Ingredients

3 cups flour

4 tsp baking powder

1 tsp salt

⅓ cup cold butter

1¼ cup milk

½ cup brown sugar

½ cup white sugar

1 tsp cinnamon

6 Tbsp butter, melted

Tip

For a delicious dessert, warm some leftover monkey bread in the microwave and top it with a scoop of ice cream.

Ingredients

Small (10 oz) loaf of French bread, pulled apart into 1-inch pieces

⅓ cup brown sugar

¾ tsp cinnamon

Dash of salt

6 large eggs

1¼ cups milk

1 tsp vanilla extract

Tip

To change it up, try using a loaf of raisin bread instead of French bread.

Tiana's Baked Caramel French Toast

Serves 8 to 10

This sweet French toast dish is a big hit with the customers at Tiana's Palace. Every night, Tiana mixes up a big batch so it will be all ready to pop in the oven the next morning.

Directions

1. Generously butter a 9- x 13-inch casserole dish. Place the bread pieces in the dish.

2. In a small bowl, mix together the brown sugar, cinnamon, and salt. Sprinkle the mixture over the bread.

3. In a mixing bowl, whisk together the eggs, milk, and vanilla extract. Pour the egg mixture evenly over the bread. Then use a spatula to press the bread down to make sure it is well coated.

4. Cover the baking pan with aluminum foil and refrigerate it for at least 4 hours, or overnight.

5. When you're ready to cook the French toast, heat the oven to 350°F. Ask an adult to help you with the oven. Bake the French toast with the foil in place for 20 minutes. Remove the foil, and continue baking for another 25 minutes.

6. Take the tray out of the oven and let cool for about 5 minutes before serving.

Lunch

Belle's Corn Chowder

Serves 4 to 6

Topped with bits of bacon, this hearty soup is one of Belle and the Beast's favorite ways to warm up after a snowball fight!

Directions

1. Peel off the onion's hard outer layer, and cut the onion into ½-inch pieces. Then chop the red potatoes into bite-size cubes. Set the onion and potatoes aside.

2. Melt the butter in a heavy saucepan over medium-low heat. Cook the onion in the melted butter until the onion starts to turn clear (about 3 or 4 minutes).

3. Add the potatoes and water, then cover the pan and let simmer for 15 minutes.

4. Stir in the whole-kernel corn, creamed corn, milk, salt, and pepper. Continue cooking and stirring the chowder until it heats through (about 7 minutes).

5. Ladle the chowder into bowls, sprinkle bacon bits on top, and serve.

Ingredients

1 medium onion

2 medium red potatoes

2 Tbsp butter

1 cup water

2 cups whole-kernel corn

1½ cups creamed corn

1½ cups milk

½ tsp salt

Dash of pepper

5 Tbsp bacon bits

Tip

Try this soup with Belle's Bonjour Baguette (p. 82) for a delicious combination.

Ingredients

1 head of lettuce

1 cup shredded carrot

15 cucumber slices

9 cherry tomatoes, halved

Citrus Dressing

½ cup orange juice

2 Tbsp lemon juice

1 Tbsp vegetable oil

1 Tbsp honey

Tip

Sweeten up your salad by sprinkling sliced almonds and fresh fruit on top.

Cinderella's All-Dressed-Up Salad

Makes 3

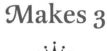

Cinderella's fairy godmother can transform a pumpkin into a coach, mice into horses, and rags into a beautiful dress. So it's no surprise that Cinderella would find a way to turn a few simple ingredients into an amazing salad dressing.

Directions

1. Rinse the lettuce well with cold water, and then pat the leaves dry with paper towels. Tear the lettuce into bite-size pieces and put an equal amount on 3 salad plates.

2. On each plate, top the lettuce with ⅓ cup shredded carrot, 5 cucumber slices, and 3 cherry tomatoes.

3. In a small bowl, whisk together the orange juice, lemon juice, vegetable oil, and honey.

4. Spoon dressing onto each salad, and serve.

Ham and Cheese Biscuit Braids

Makes 16

It only takes a quick look around the tower to realize what an amazing artist Rapunzel is. Her creativity goes beyond the paintings on the walls, though. It shows up in her cooking, too!

Directions

1. Heat the oven to 400°F.

2. In a mixing bowl, stir together the flour, cornmeal, baking powder, and salt.

3. Use your fingertips to pinch the butter into the flour mixture until the bits are the size of peas. Stir in the ham and cheese. Add the milk, and stir the mixture just until it starts to look doughy.

4. Sprinkle some flour onto a cutting board and set the dough on top. Sprinkle a little more flour on the dough to keep it from sticking. Using a rolling pin, flatten the dough into a 12-inch square. The dough should be between a ¼-inch and ½-inch thick.

5. Slice the square into quarters. Then slice each quarter into 12 strips, each about 6 inches long.

6. Now it's time to braid the dough. Gather 3 strips, and pinch them together at the top. Take the right section and cross it over the center section so that they switch places. Then, take the left section and cross it over the center section. Keep going until the whole strip is braided, then pinch the strands together at the bottom. Repeat until you've braided all the strips.

7. Ask an adult to help you with the oven. Place the braids, spaced apart, on an ungreased baking sheet. Bake them until the dough starts to turn golden brown (about 8 to 10 minutes).

Ingredients

2 cups flour

½ cup cornmeal

3 tsp baking powder

1 tsp salt

5 Tbsp cold butter, cut into several pieces

½ cup diced ham

½ cup shredded cheddar cheese

1 cup milk

Tip

You can use grated Parmesan or Romano cheese instead of cheddar, if you like.

Ingredients

1 medium English cucumber

3 Tbsp rice wine vinegar

1 Tbsp sugar

1 Tbsp toasted sesame seeds

Salt to taste

Dash crushed red pepper flakes (optional)

Tip

Red pepper flakes are really spicy, so don't use too many—unless you want to breathe fire like Mushu!

Cri-Kee's Lucky Cucumber Salad

Serves 6 to 8

Mulan's cricket friend, Cri-Kee, loves spending time in the Fa family garden. After catching the shy insect nibbling on a cucumber, Mulan decided to name this crunchy salad after him.

Directions

1. Cut the cucumber into thin, circular slices.

2. In a medium-size bowl, stir together the cucumber slices, vinegar, sugar, sesame seeds, and salt. Add the crushed red pepper flakes if you're using them.

3. Chill the cucumber salad for 30 minutes before serving.

Pasta Shell Salad

Serves 8 to 10

Ariel thinks this colorful combination of garden veggies and shell-shaped pasta is the perfect mix of land and sea.

Directions

1. Prepare the pasta according to the directions on the box.

2. In a large bowl, combine the cooked pasta shells, red pepper, carrots, cherry tomatoes, Parmesan, and chives. Stir with a wooden spoon to mix them.

3. Pour the Italian salad dressing over the pasta, and sprinkle on the salt and pepper. Stir again until all the ingredients are evenly coated.

4. Cover the bowl with plastic wrap and chill until serving time.

Ingredients

1 (16 oz) box of pasta shells

½ cup diced red bell pepper

½ cup shredded carrots

½ cup halved cherry tomatoes

¼ cup grated Parmesan cheese

2 Tbsp snipped chives

1 cup Italian salad dressing

¼ tsp salt

¼ tsp ground pepper

Tip

Cubed mozzarella cheese and pepperoni slices make great additions to this salad.

1 carrot

Half of a red bell pepper

2 flatbreads or
large flour tortillas

Cream-cheese spread
(plain or veggie)

Tip

You can make these
roll-ups using hummus
instead of cream cheese.
Try Jasmine's Homemade
Hummus on p. 94!

Magic Carpet Roll-Ups
Makes 2

Brightly trimmed with carrot and red-pepper tassels, these roll-up sandwiches are Jasmine's top choice for lunch on the fly.

Directions

1. Ask an adult to help you prepare the vegetables. Peel the carrot and slice it into 3-inch-long sections. Cut each section into thin strips. Slice the red bell pepper into similarly sized strips.

2. Trim off the curved edges of each flatbread or tortilla to create a rectangular "carpet" shape.

3. Spread cream cheese on the surface of each flatbread, and then roll it up.

4. Add "tassels" to each Magic-Carpet sandwich by inserting several of the carrot and red-pepper strips into the center coil at both ends.

Tiana's Tasty Sandwiches

Makes 8 to 12

Tiana and Naveen love to make these flower-shaped sandwiches for lunch. To make them extra tasty, Tiana seasons the mayonnaise with a few secret ingredients.

Directions

1. In a small bowl, stir together the mayonnaise, garlic powder, and paprika.

2. For each sandwich, use a large, flower-shaped cookie cutter (about 3 inches wide) to cut the center from a slice of white bread. Next, cut a matching flower shape from a slice of wheat bread.

3. Use a small, round cookie cutter (about 1¼ inches wide) to cut a hole in the middle of each bread flower cutout. Place the center of the wheat flower into the white flower and the center of the white flower into the wheat flower.

4. Cut flower shapes from slices of ham and cheese (but don't cut holes in the centers).

5. Spread mayonnaise mixture on one of the bread flowers, and layer on the ham and cheese cutouts. Top off the sandwich with the second bread flower. You can spread a little more mayonnaise on this layer too, if you like.

Ingredients

¼ cup mayonnaise

¼ tsp garlic powder

¼ tsp paprika

White bread and wheat bread (1 slice of each per sandwich)

Sliced ham

Sliced cheese

Tip

You can make any shape sandwich you want by using different cookie cutters.

1 carrot

2 stalks celery

1 qt chicken broth

1 cooked chicken breast,
cut into small pieces
(about 1 packed cup)

½ cup uncooked ditalini
or similar pasta

Salt and pepper to taste

For a simpler soup, bring
the broth to a simmer
and stir in 1 cup frozen
mixed vegetables in place
of the carrot and celery.

Seven Dwarfs' Soup

Serves 3 to 4

Made with seven tasty ingredients—one for each of the dwarfs—this recipe adds up to one delicious meal. Careful! The pepper might make you Sneezy. . . .

Directions

1. Peel the carrot and cut it into thin slices. Prepare your celery stalks by slicing off the leafy tops and white bottoms. Cut the remaining stalks into thin slices.

2. Ask an adult to help you combine the chicken broth, carrot slices, and celery slices in a large saucepan. Cook over high heat until the broth begins to bubble. Turn the heat down to low and let simmer for 3 minutes.

3. Stir in the chicken and pasta. Continue simmering the soup until the pasta is cooked al dente (about 10 more minutes).

4. Season the soup with salt and ground pepper, and serve.

Bull's-Eye Pizza

Makes 2

Nothing's more important to Princess Merida than being able to make your own choices. That's why this pizza recipe is all about targeting the toppings you like best.

Directions

1. Divide the pizza dough in half and knead each piece into a ball. Place dough balls in a large bowl and cover both with plastic wrap. Let them rest at room temperature for 10 minutes.

2. Heat the oven to 425°F. Lightly oil two baking sheets and sprinkle a pinch or two of cornmeal on top.

3. Working on a flour-dusted surface, roll both dough balls into ¼-inch-thick circles. Carefully place each one on a prepared baking sheet.

4. Spread spoonfuls of pizza sauce on both pizza crusts. Top the sauce with grated mozzarella cheese.

5. Add your choice of toppings. Place one kind—chopped ham or pepperoni slices, for example—in the center. Arrange a second topping in a ring around the first one. Keep adding toppings in this way, creating a colorful bull's-eye pattern, until you reach the crust.

6. Ask an adult to help you with the oven. Bake the pizzas on different oven racks until the edges and bottoms of the crusts are golden brown (about 15 minutes). Switch the position of the trays after 7 or 8 minutes so that the pizzas will cook evenly.

7. Let the cooked pizzas cool slightly before slicing and serving.

Ingredients

16 oz premade
pizza dough

1 tablespoon olive oil

2 pinches cornmeal

1 cup pizza sauce

2 cups grated
mozzarella cheese

Toppings

Diced ham

Pepperoni

Broccoli florets

Diced bell peppers

Pineapple chunks

Sliced black olives

Tip

If you use pineapple chunks for a topping, blot them first with a paper towel to absorb extra juice and keep the crust from getting soggy.

Ingredients

1 cup sliced strawberries

3 Tbsp cold water

2 tsp cornstarch

2 Tbsp sugar

Tip

Remove strawberry leaves by pushing the end of a drinking straw into the bottom tip of the berry and through its center until the top pops off.

Aurora's Homemade Jam

Makes ½ cup

Aurora loves spending time with her forest friends, especially when they go berry picking. The birds and squirrels show her where to find the best berry bushes! Back at the cottage, Aurora uses their sweet discoveries to make this yummy sandwich spread.

Directions

1. Put the strawberries in a medium-size heavy saucepan. Use a potato masher or fork to crush them up.

2. In a small bowl, mix the cold water and cornstarch together. Then mix in the sugar.

3. Combine the cornstarch mixture with the strawberries in the saucepan. Heat on medium-low until the mixture starts to bubble. Then turn the heat down to low and cook for 4 to 5 minutes, stirring all the while.

4. Remove the pan from the heat and set aside until the jam cools.

Dinner

Ingredients

1 cup butter cracker crumbs

⅓ cup grated
Parmesan cheese

½ tsp garlic powder

½ tsp paprika

¼ tsp salt

¼ tsp ground pepper

2 eggs

2 Tbsp water

1 Tbsp honey

1½ lb chicken tenders

Tip

Serve your chicken
tenders with honey-
mustard or barbecue
sauce for dipping.

Cozy Cottage Chicken Tenders

Serves 6

The good fairy Fauna was never very good at cooking. Luckily, this scrumptious recipe is so easy, even she can make it—without a magic wand!

Directions

1. Heat the oven to 400°F. Line a baking sheet with parchment paper.

2. Combine the cracker crumbs, Parmesan, garlic powder, paprika, salt, and pepper in a sealable, gallon-size plastic bag.

3. In a medium-size bowl, whisk together the eggs, water, and honey.

4. Rinse the chicken tenders with cold water and then pat them dry with paper towels. Place the tenders in the egg mixture so that they are completely covered.

5. Use a fork to transfer 2 or 3 tenders to the bag of cracker crumbs. Seal the bag, and shake. Arrange the coated chicken pieces on the baking sheet. Repeat this step until all the tenders are coated and on the sheet.

6. Ask an adult to help you with the oven. Bake the chicken for 10 minutes. Then turn the pieces over and continue baking until they are cooked through (another 10 minutes or so).

Hoppin' John

Serves 6 to 8

♔ ♔ ♔ ♔ ♔

Made with black-eyed peas, ham, and rice, this popular Southern dish is supposed to bring good luck if you eat it on New Year's Day. But it tastes so good, Tiana keeps it on the menu all year long.

Directions

1. Rinse the black-eyed peas in a metal strainer, then put them in a large saucepan.

2. Pour in 4 cups of the water. Bring the beans to a boil and cook them for 2 minutes. Then remove the pan from the heat and let the beans stand for 1 hour.

3. Melt the butter in a large skillet over low heat. Add the ham, onion, celery, carrots, garlic, celery salt, red pepper flakes, and pepper. Cook the mixture until it heats through and the onion starts to look clear (about 6 to 8 minutes).

4. Add the beans and their liquid to the skillet and stir. Bring the mixture to a boil, and then lower the heat until the cooking slows down to a simmer. Cover the pan and continue cooking until the beans are tender, about 6 to 8 minutes.

5. Pour in 1 more cup of water, and stir in the rice. Re-cover the skillet and continue simmering for about 20 minutes, or until the rice is cooked.

6. Drain off any extra liquid, give the Hoppin' John a final stir, and serve.

Ingredients

½ lb dried black-eyed peas

4 cups water

1 Tbsp butter

½ lb baked ham, cubed

1 medium onion, chopped

2 stalks celery, chopped

2 medium carrots, chopped

2 cloves garlic, minced

¼ tsp celery salt

¼ tsp red pepper flakes

Dash of pepper

1 cup water

1 cup long grain white rice

Tip

When you rinse the peas, be sure to sort through them for any loose pebbles that might have been mixed in by mistake when they were picked.

3 tsp vegetable oil

1 tsp ginger powder

4 cups broccoli slaw mix

1 lb pork tenderloin, cooked and sliced

¼ cup hoisin sauce

Salt to taste

Flour tortillas, warmed

Tip

You can add a little extra hoisin sauce before serving, if you like.

Mushu's Moo Shu

Serves 4 to 6

Mulan's dragon companion, Mushu, makes sure she has plenty to eat on tough training days. This delicious dish is fun and filling for any princess on the go!

Directions

1. Ask an adult to help you at the stove. Heat the oil in a large, nonstick frying pan or wok over medium-high heat. Add the ginger powder and stir for 1 minute.

2. Add the broccoli slaw to the pan, and turn up the heat a little. Stir-fry the vegetables for 4 to 5 minutes. Cook them just long enough to darken in color without losing their crunchiness.

3. Turn the heat down to medium, and stir in the pork and hoisin sauce. Continue cooking the moo shu for another 2 minutes to heat it through. Add salt to taste.

4. When you're ready to eat, spoon some of the moo shu onto the center of a warm tortilla. Then roll or wrap up the tortilla, and enjoy.

Bayou Meatloaf

Serves 6 to 8

♛ ♛ ♛ ♛

Louis the alligator loves playing his trumpet at Tiana's restaurant—almost as much as he loves eating this yummy meatloaf after a show!

Directions

1. Heat the oven to 350°F. Grease the bottom and sides of a 2½-quart casserole dish.

2. Combine the ground beef and ground pork in a large mixing bowl.

3. In a small bowl or cup, stir together the celery salt, garlic powder, thyme, paprika, and pepper. Sprinkle the mixture over the meat.

4. Add the bread crumbs, onion, ketchup, milk, and eggs to the meat. Use a wooden spoon to stir all the ingredients together until they are well mixed. Pack the meatloaf mixture into the casserole dish.

5. Ask an adult to help you with the oven. Place the meatloaf in the oven and bake for 50 minutes. Then carefully remove it from the oven. Spread the ketchup topping on top using a wooden spatula. Return the meatloaf to the oven to bake for 10 more minutes.

6. Let the meatloaf cool for a few minutes before you slice and serve it.

Ingredients

Meatloaf

1 lb ground beef (85% to 90% lean)

1 lb ground pork

1 tsp celery salt

1 tsp garlic powder

1 tsp dried thyme

1 tsp paprika

¼ tsp pepper

1 cup bread crumbs

½ cup minced onion

½ cup ketchup

½ cup milk

2 large eggs, lightly beaten

Topping

½ cup ketchup with 1 Tbsp honey stirred in

Tip

Leftover meatloaf tastes great in a sandwich, especially if you toast the bread.

Ingredients

1 egg

1½ cups flaked cooked cod fillets (about 12 oz)

5 Tbsp Italian-style bread crumbs

2 Tbsp mayonnaise

1 Tbsp lime juice

¼ tsp paprika

¼ tsp celery salt

Dash of pepper

3 tsp vegetable oil

½ tsp butter

Tip

Make your own yummy dipping sauce by stirring a little lime juice and a dash of celery salt into a large spoonful of mayonnaise.

Un*bear*ably Delicious Fish Cakes

Makes 6

♛ ♛ ♛

Merida and Queen Elinor love making these fish cakes as a reminder of their adventure together. Of course, now that Merida's mum isn't a bear anymore, she prefers her fish cooked!

Directions

1. In a large bowl, crack the egg and beat it with a whisk.

2. Break up the cod fillets into bite-size pieces, and mix with the eggs. Then add the bread crumbs, mayonnaise, lime juice, paprika, celery salt, and pepper. Mix well with a rubber spatula.

3. Cover the bowl with plastic wrap and chill for 15 minutes in the refrigerator.

4. Ask an adult for help at the stove. Heat the vegetable oil and butter in a frying pan on medium low. When the butter starts to bubble, spoon six equal mounds of the fish cake mixture into the pan. Press down on them lightly with the back of the spoon to flatten the tops.

5. Cook the fish cakes for 3 to 4 minutes on each side, then serve.

Gus's Mac and Cheeseburger

Serves 4 to 6

Named after one of Cinderella's biggest little fans, this saucy supper has Gus's favorite cheese plus a few other flavorful ingredients: bite-size bits of burger and a buttery cracker topping.

Directions

1. Cook the macaroni according to the directions on the box.

2. Ask an adult to help you at the stove. Place the ground beef in a heavy saucepan and cook over medium heat. Make sure to cook the beef until it is completely brown, then drain off any liquid.

3. Heat the oven to 350°F. Combine the hamburger and the cooked macaroni in a 2½ or 3-quart casserole dish.

4. Melt the 4 tablespoons of butter in a heavy saucepan over medium heat. Stir the flour into the butter with a wooden spoon. As soon as the sauce starts to bubble, add the milk, mustard, and nutmeg, and whisk until the mixture is blended.

5. Stir in the cheese, and continue stirring until it is completely melted and the sauce starts to thicken.

6. Ladle the cheese sauce into the casserole dish, and gently stir until the macaroni and hamburger are evenly coated.

7. Mix all the topping ingredients together in a bowl and then sprinkle them on the macaroni.

8. Ask an adult to help you with the oven. Put the casserole dish in the oven. Bake the macaroni and cheese until it heats all the way through and starts to bubble (about 20 to 25 minutes). Let cool slightly before serving.

Ingredients

1 (16 oz) elbow macaroni

½ lb ground beef

4 Tbsp butter

3 Tbsp flour

2½ cups milk

1 Tbsp mustard

Dash of nutmeg

4 cups shredded sharp cheddar cheese

Topping

2 Tbsp butter, melted

½ cup bread crumbs or cracker crumbs

⅛ tsp paprika

Tip

Get creative! Try mixing and matching different kinds of cheese for this recipe.

8 oz spaghetti

1 tsp dark sesame oil

2 Tbsp canola oil

3 cups chopped
fresh broccoli

½ red bell pepper,
cut into thin strips

1½ tsp ground ginger

½ tsp garlic powder

1 lb sirloin tips,
thinly sliced

¼ cup beef broth

¼ tsp soy sauce

2 Tbsp brown sugar

Tip

You can make lo mein
with all kinds of
vegetables, including
peas, carrots, bok
choy, water chestnuts,
and mushrooms.

Fa Family Lo Mein

Serves 4 to 6

The Fa family loves to share a big bowl of lo mein at dinnertime. Made with spaghetti and fresh veggies, this spin on the traditional noodle dish is fun to eat with chopsticks.

Directions

1. Cook the spaghetti according to the directions on the package, and then drain it. Return it to the pot. Drizzle the sesame oil over the pasta, and stir gently until the noodles are evenly coated. Set the pasta aside.

2. Ask an adult to help you at the stove. Heat the canola oil in a large skillet or a wok over medium-high heat. Add the broccoli and red pepper and cook for 3 minutes, stirring all the while. Stir in the ground ginger and garlic powder.

3. Add the sirloin tips. Cook and stir the mixture until the meat is no longer pink (about 5 minutes).

4. In a small bowl, stir together the broth, soy sauce, and brown sugar. Add the broth mixture and the pasta to the pan. Continue cooking and stirring the lo mein until it is heated through. Serve immediately.

Magic Lamp Curry

Serves 4

Just like Aladdin's friend the Genie, this spicy, golden curry sauce can fulfill three dinner wishes. You can make it with chicken (simply follow the recipe) or beef (substitute ½ lb of sliced sirloin tips for the chicken). Or, for a yummy veggie version, leave out the meat and double the spinach.

Directions

1. Ask an adult to help you at the stove. Heat the vegetable oil in a large frying pan over high heat. Cook the chicken and onion in the pan, stirring often, for 6 to 7 minutes to lightly brown the meat. Transfer the chicken and onion to a bowl, and set it aside.

2. Pour any leftover liquid out of the pan and into a leak-proof container. Turn the heat down to low, and melt the butter in the pan. Stir in the curry and garlic powder, and cook until the mixture starts to bubble (about 1 or 2 minutes).

3. Stir in the coconut milk, raisins, and grated apple. Then add the chicken and onion back in. Cover the pan and simmer the chicken curry for 10 minutes.

4. Stir in the fresh baby spinach and simmer for 2 more minutes. Serve the curry on its own or with rice.

Ingredients

1 Tbsp vegetable oil

1 chicken breast, cut into bite-size pieces

1 onion, chopped

2 Tbsp butter

1½ Tbsp curry powder

¼ tsp garlic powder

1 (13.5 oz) can coconut milk

½ cup raisins

½ apple, peeled and grated

1 packed cup fresh baby spinach

Tip

If you like your curry extra spicy, try adding another ½ Tbsp of curry powder.

Ingredients

2 Tbsp butter

1 medium onion, chopped

1 stalk celery, chopped

1½ lb ground beef

¼ tsp garlic powder

3 Tbsp flour

1 cup beef broth

1 (14.5 oz) can
diced tomatoes

1 tsp dried thyme

½ tsp dried rosemary

1½ cups corn kernels

5 cups warm
mashed potatoes

Paprika

Tip

It takes about
6 medium-large
potatoes to make
5 cups of mashed
potatoes.

Savory Shepherd's Pie

Serves 6 to 8

♔ ♔ ♔ ♔ ♔

Lords Macintosh, MacGuffin, and Dingwall are always arguing! So to keep them quiet at dinner, Merida and Queen Elinor make a delicious shepherd's pie. This tasty dish is the one thing they can all agree on.

Directions

1. Ask an adult to help you at the stove. Melt the butter in a large frying pan over medium heat. Add the onion and celery, and sauté them for 5 minutes, stirring often.

2. Add the ground beef to the pan, and break it up with a wooden spoon or spatula. Cook the meat, stirring and turning it over every so often, until it browns. Then lower the heat, and carefully spoon out any excess fat from the cooking liquid.

3. Stir the garlic and flour into the beef. Add the beef broth, diced tomatoes, thyme, rosemary, and corn. Gently stir all the ingredients until they are well combined.

4. Bring the mixture to a simmer, and cook for 3 or 4 minutes. Then spoon it into a large, greased casserole dish.

5. Heat the oven to 400°F. Spread the warm mashed potatoes on top of the meat and corn. Sprinkle the top with paprika.

6. Bake the shepherd's pie until it heats all the way through and the top turns golden brown (about 25 minutes). Let cool for 10 minutes before serving.

The Beast's Quiche

Serves 6 to 8

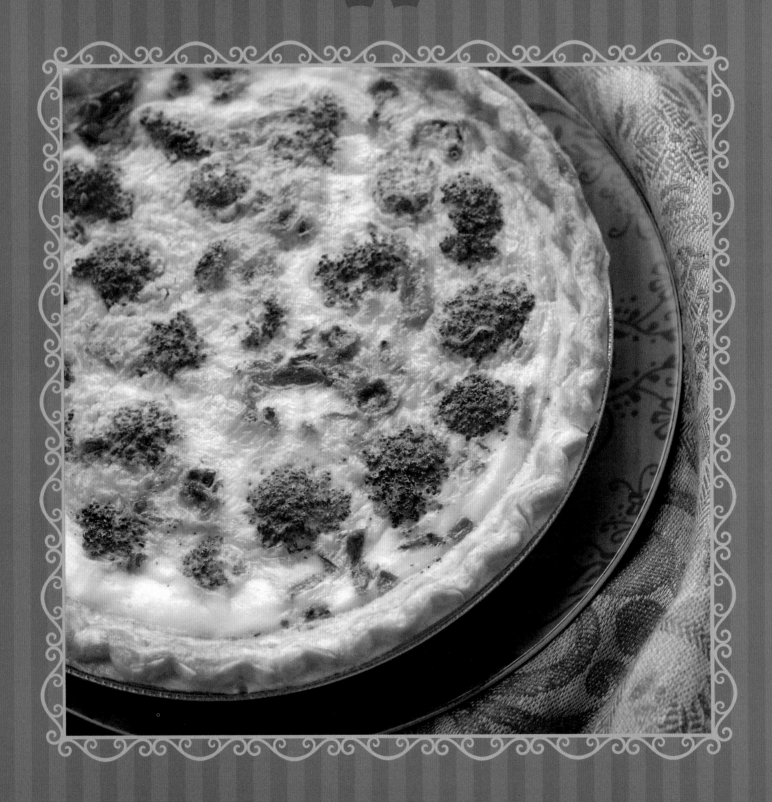

Before Belle arrived at the castle, the Beast ate with his paws! But with a little coaching, he quickly learned how to eat more elegant meals—like this bacon and broccoli quiche—with a fork.

Directions

1. Heat the oven to 425°F.

2. Set the pie shell in its pan on a heavy baking sheet. (This will make it easier to move once you fill it.) Loosely cover the outer edge of the pie shell with strips of aluminum foil to keep it from browning too quickly in the oven.

3. Sprinkle the cheese evenly across the bottom of the pie shell. Add the crumbled bacon and broccoli florets.

4. In a large mixing bowl, whisk together the eggs, milk, and pepper until they are well mixed. Pour the mixture over the other ingredients in the pie shell.

5. Ask an adult to help you with the oven. Bake the quiche for 15 minutes. Then reduce the heat to 325°F. Carefully remove the aluminum foil from the edge of the shell, and continue baking for 25 minutes.

6. Let the quiche cool slightly before serving.

Ingredients

Premade frozen
9-inch pie shell

1 cup grated
cheddar cheese

4 strips cooked
bacon, crumbled

1 cup cooked
broccoli florets

4 eggs

1 cup milk

¼ tsp pepper

Tip

You can eat quiche anytime—for breakfast, lunch, or dinner!

Sides

⤞⧉⤝

Southern Spoon Bread

Serves 6 to 8

Tiana loves adding her own spin to her favorite dishes. This spoon bread tastes a lot like cornbread, but it has a delicious gooey texture that's fun to spoon up at mealtime.

Directions

1. Heat the oven to 375°. Butter a 2-quart casserole dish.

2. Ask an adult to help you at the stove. Heat the milk and water in a large, heavy saucepan over medium heat. Turn the heat to low as soon as bubbles form against the pan (before the milk boils). Add the butter and salt, and stir until the butter melts.

3. Slowly whisk the cornmeal into the milk. Keep whisking just until the mixture thickens (about 1 minute). Remove the pan from the heat and let the cornmeal cool a bit.

4. Next, separate the egg yolks and the egg whites into different bowls.

5. Beat the egg whites with a mixer until they are foamy and stiff, and set them aside.

6. Beat together the yolks, honey, and baking powder with a fork or whisk. Then whisk the mixture into the cornmeal. Pour the cornmeal mixture into the bowl of beaten egg whites.

7. Use a rubber spatula to gently fold the egg whites into the cornmeal.

8. Scrape the spoon bread batter into the casserole dish. Ask an adult to help you put the dish in the oven. Bake it until the top turns golden brown and a toothpick inserted in the middle comes out clean (about 25 to 30 minutes). Serve the spoon bread warm, scooping it out of the casserole dish with a big spoon.

Ingredients

2 cups milk

1 cup water

1 Tbsp butter

1 tsp salt

1 cup cornmeal

2 eggs

2 Tbsp honey

2½ tsp baking powder

Tip

Not sure how to separate egg whites and yolks? Check out the Glossary (p. 139)!

Ingredients

2 medium-size
sweet potatoes,
peeled and sliced
about ¼-inch thick

1 Tbsp vegetable oil
or olive oil

Salt and pepper to taste

Tip

You can use different
cookie cutters, such
as stars or hearts, to
make fun shapes, too!

Sweet Potato Coins

Serves 2 to 3

These sweet-and-salty oven fries remind Aladdin of the golden coins he discovered in the Cave of Wonders. But these coins are much tastier!

Directions

1. Heat the oven to 400°F. Use small, round cookie cutter (up to 2 inches wide or so) to cut out a bunch of "coins" from the sweet potato slices. To make it extra easy, place the flat end of a wooden spoon on top of the cutter, and press down on the spoon.

2. Put the potato coins in a mixing bowl. Drizzle the oil on top, and stir with a wooden spoon until the coins are evenly coated.

3. Line a baking sheet with aluminum foil. Then, place the coins on the sheet, spacing them slightly apart. Sprinkle on salt and pepper.

4. Ask an adult to help you with the oven. Bake the coins until the bottoms are golden brown, about 10 to 12 minutes. Remove them from the oven, and use a spatula to flip them over. Bake the coins for another 10 to 12 minutes.

Confetti Corn

Serves 6

$\mathcal{M}$ade with red pepper, yellow corn, and fresh green basil, this colorful medley is as festive as the Mardi Gras Parade!

Directions

1. Ask an adult to help you at the stove. Heat the vegetable oil in a medium-size frying pan over medium-low heat. Sauté the diced red pepper in the oil for 2 minutes.

2. Add the corn, crumbled bacon, basil, and butter. Stir the ingredients together, and cook them until they are hot and well mixed and the butter is melted.

3. Remove the pan from the heat. Stir in salt and pepper to taste.

Ingredients

1 tsp vegetable oil

½ cup diced red bell pepper

2 cups cooked corn

3 strips cooked bacon, crumbled

1 tsp dried basil

½ tsp butter

Salt and pepper to taste

Tip

Leftover cooked sweet corn, cut off the cob, tastes especially good in this recipe.

½ cup warm water

1 package active dry yeast

1½ cups water
(at room temperature)

1½ tsp salt

4½ cups flour

2 Tbsp cornmeal

1 Tbsp milk

Tip

Try this bread with
Aurora's Homemade
Jam (p. 50)!

Belle's Bonjour Baguette

Makes 2

One of Belle's favorite shops is the bakery. The best time to get there is bright and early, when the baker first takes the fresh baguettes out of the oven.

Directions

1. Pour the ½ cup of warm water into a mixing bowl, and sprinkle the yeast on top. Once the yeast dissolves, stir in the 1½ cups of water, the salt, and 4 cups of the flour.

2. Sprinkle the remaining ½ cup of flour onto a cutting board, and turn the dough out onto it. Knead the dough until all the flour is mixed in. Put the dough in a greased bowl, and cover it with a damp paper towel. Set the bowl aside in a warm spot until the dough doubles in size (about 1 hour).

3. Sprinkle the cornmeal onto a large baking sheet. Punch down the dough and then divide it into halves. Shape each half into a 12-inch-long fat rope, and place them on the baking sheet.

4. Cut a few ¼-inch-deep diagonal slits in the top of each loaf. Cover the bread with damp paper towels, and set it aside to rise for 1 hour.

5. Heat the oven to 400°F. Use a pastry brush to lightly brush the top of each loaf with milk. Ask an adult to help you place the pan in the oven. Bake the bread until it turns golden brown, 20 to 25 minutes.

Triple-licious Fruit Salad

Serves 6 to 8

There's nothing that Merida's brothers Harris, Hubert, and Hamish like to stir up more than trouble—except maybe this sweet and juicy tricolored treat.

Directions

1. Use a melon baller to scoop 1 dozen balls from each melon half, and combine them all in a big bowl.

2. Gently stir the melon balls with a wooden spoon so that the colors are evenly mixed.

3. Spoon your fruit salad into small serving dishes, and enjoy! Cover any leftover fruit salad with plastic wrap, and chill it in the refrigerator until you're ready for more.

Half of a cantaloupe

Half of a honeydew melon

Half of a small seedless watermelon

Tip

This summertime salad is even more refreshing when served with snipped mint.

½ lb snow peas

1 Tbsp water

1 tsp butter

Dinglehopper Snow Peas

Serves 3 to 4

Ariel loves to use her dinglehopper—what humans call a fork—to eat these deliciously crunchy veggies.

Directions

1. Rinse the snow peas well in cold water. Then snap off the top of each pod, pulling it downward to remove the strings along the sides.

2. Place the prepared pods and the tablespoon of water in a microwavable casserole dish. Cover the dish, and microwave the peas on high for 3 minutes.

3. Use potholders to remove the casserole dish from the microwave. Add butter to the peas, gently stir, and serve.

Tip

For a zestier dish, drizzle ½ teaspoon or so of Italian dressing on the snow peas instead of butter.

Snacks

1 cup whipped
cream cheese

1 cup sour cream

2 tsp dried dill weed

1 Tbsp garlic powder

¼ tsp salt

Baby carrots

Tip

This dip tastes great
with celery, too!

Maximus's Baby Carrots and Dip

Makes 2 cups

*A*s head of the Royal Guard, Maximus is treated to all the carrots he likes, served with a delicious dip, of course.

Directions

1. In a medium-size bowl, stir together the whipped cream cheese and sour cream until well blended. Then stir in the dill weed, garlic powder, and salt.

2. Chill the dip for at least 30 minutes. Serve it with plenty of baby carrots.

Under the Sea Sand Dollar Crackers

Makes 4 dozen

Human items aren't the only treasures Ariel likes to collect. These homemade crackers are inspired by the beautiful sand dollars she finds on the beach.

Directions

1. Heat the oven to 400°F. Line a large baking sheet with parchment paper.

2. In a mixing bowl, whisk together the flour, Parmesan cheese, salt, and paprika. Add the butter pieces to the flour mixture, and use your fingers to pinch them until the bits are the size of small peas.

3. Add the half-and-half and stir until the dough pulls together. Turn the dough onto a lightly floured surface, and knead it a few times.

4. Use a floured rolling pin to roll the cracker dough very thin (about ⅛-inch thick). With a round cookie cutter (about 2¼ inches wide), cut out a bunch of circles from the dough. Arrange the dough circles, spaced apart, on the baking sheet. Gather the dough scraps and knead them together, then reroll the dough so you can cut more circles from it.

5. Use the tip of a toothpick or wooden kitchen skewer to poke through the center of each dough circle, and wiggle it around to make a small hole (this helps keep the cracker flat when it bakes).

6. Working with one cracker at a time, use a pastry brush to spread a tiny bit of water on top. Then lightly press 5 almond slices into the dough around the hole to create a star shape.

7. Ask an adult to help you with the oven. Bake the crackers until they start to brown on top, about 6 to 7 minutes. Remove them from the oven and transfer them to a wire rack to cool for a bit before you eat them.

Ingredients

1¼ cups flour

⅓ cup grated Parmesan cheese

½ tsp salt

½ tsp paprika

3 Tbsp cold butter, cut into pieces

½ cup half-and-half

Sliced almonds

Tip

If you want to make the crackers without almonds, you can simply use a toothpick to poke a sand-dollar pattern in the dough.

Ingredients

1 (15 oz) can
garbanzo beans

¼ cup olive oil

2 Tbsp lemon juice

¼ tsp garlic powder

¼ tsp salt

Pita bread

Tip

There are lots of fun
ways to eat hummus.
Try it on pretzels, fresh
veggies—even bagels!

Jasmine's Homemade Hummus

Makes 2 cups

Flavored with lemon and garlic, this tasty chickpea spread is
a staple in the Sultan's palace kitchen.

Directions

1. Drain the garbanzo beans and combine
   with the olive oil, lemon juice, garlic
   powder, and salt in the bowl of a
   food processor or blender.

2. Blend ingredients until smooth.

3. Spoon the hummus into a
   small bowl. Serve with pita
   bread triangles.

Princess Pink Popcorn

Serves 3 to 4

As far as the good fairy Flora is concerned, everything—from birthday dresses to popcorn—looks pretty in pink.

Directions

1. Put the popped popcorn in a large mixing bowl, removing any unpopped kernels.

2. Ask an adult to help you at the stove. Melt the butter in a medium-size saucepan over medium-low heat. Add the marshmallows and stir continually until they melt and turn into a smooth sauce. Stir in the strawberry gelatin powder. Use a plastic spoon for this step. (The pink gelatin can stain a wooden spoon.)

3. Immediately pour the pink marshmallow over the popcorn, and gently stir to evenly cover the kernels.

4. Let the popcorn cool for a few minutes before serving.

Ingredients

Bag of popped microwave popcorn (about 6 cups)

2½ Tbsp butter

18 large marshmallows

3 Tbsp strawberry-flavored gelatin powder

Tip

Melted marshmallow is hot, so be sure to use a long-handled spoon to stir it.

8 large strawberries

Whipped cream

Tip

A strawberry rose makes the perfect topping for a bowl of yogurt, too.

Enchanting Strawberry Roses

Serves 4

Of all the magnificent desserts served in the enchanted castle, this beautiful berry blossom is one of Belle's favorites.

Directions

1. Wash the strawberries in cold water and pat them dry with a paper towel.

2. Ask an adult to help you with the knife. Then, slice off the strawberries' leafy tops.

3. Turn one of the strawberries upside down. Create an outer row of 4 rose petals around the tip by slicing three-quarters of the way down through the berry on all 4 sides.

4. To finish the rose, cut the second strawberry in half from top to bottom. Then cut one of the halves into several slices. Tuck 3 or 4 of the slices between the tip and outer petals of the first berry.

5. Repeat with the remaining strawberries.

6. Put a spoonful of whipped cream into the bottoms of four small bowls. Set the strawberry roses on top, and serve.

Beverages

Mrs. Potts's Raspberry-Mint Iced Tea

Serves 4

When the weather's warm, Mrs. Potts helps everyone keep cool with her delicious iced tea.

Directions

1. On the stove, heat the water until it is near boiling. Then remove from heat.

2. Steep the bags of raspberry and mint tea in the water for 4 minutes.

3. Remove the teabags and stir in the honey while the tea is still warm. Let the sweetened tea cool.

4. Fill tall glasses with plenty of ice, pour in the tea, and serve.

Ingredients

1 qt water

3 bags herbal raspberry tea

2 bags herbal mint tea

2 or 3 Tbsp honey

Ice

Tip

Just about any flavor of fruit tea works well with this recipe.

Ingredients

1 cup lemonade

1 cup orange juice

2 cups seltzer water

Ice

Tip

For a festive touch, add a slice of orange or lemon to each glass.

Sun Punch

Serves 4

This golden-yellow drink is as sparkly as the floating lanterns that light the sky on Rapunzel's birthday.

Directions

1. Stir the lemonade and orange juice together in a pitcher.

2. Slowly pour in the seltzer water.

3. Fill four tall glasses with plenty of ice. Pour in the punch, and serve.

Sweet Sea-Foam Smoothie

Serves 1

Flavored with lime and banana, Ariel loves to serve this frothy smoothie at seaside picnics.

Directions

1. Break the banana into pieces and put them into a blender.

2. Add the water, frozen yogurt, and lime juice.

3. Blend the ingredients until they are smooth and creamy.

4. Pour the smoothie into a tall glass, and serve with a straw.

1 banana

½ cup water

1 cup vanilla frozen yogurt

1 Tbsp lime juice

Tip

For a sweet switch, try making this smoothie with fresh-squeezed lemon or orange juice instead of lime juice.

Ingredients

⅓ cup white chocolate chips

⅓ cup light cream

1½ cups milk

½ tsp vanilla extract

Dash of cinnamon or nutmeg

Tip

During the holiday season, add a hint of mint by serving this drink with candy cane stirrers.

White Hot Chocolate

Serves 2

On chilly winter days, Snow White loves to warm up with this sweet and creamy white cocoa.

Directions

1. Ask an adult to help you at the stove. Mix the white chocolate chips and light cream in a small heavy saucepan. Warm the mixture over low heat until the chips melt, stirring the whole time.

2. Stir in the milk and vanilla extract. Continue stirring until the mixture is warm but not too hot. Remove the pan from the heat.

3. Whisk the white hot chocolate to make it foamy on top.

4. Spoon the foam into two large cups or mugs. Then slowly pour in the rest of the hot chocolate. Sprinkle a little cinnamon or nutmeg on top, and serve.

Sweets

Tiger-Stripe Fudge

Makes 2¼ lbs

As far as tigers go, Rajah is truly one of a kind. Not only is he protective and loyal, he also has a unique pattern of stripes. That's why this striped fudge is so much fun to make—it turns out a little different every time!

Directions

1. Heavily grease an 8- or 9-inch square pan, then line it with parchment paper.

2. Measure the semisweet chocolate chips into a small microwavable bowl or cup. Set aside for now.

3. Ask an adult to help you at the stove. Combine the sweetened condensed milk and white chocolate chips in a nonstick frying pan. Heat over medium heat, stirring continually until the chips are completely melted.

4. Add the butterscotch chips, and turn the heat down to medium-low. Continue to heat and stir the mixture until the chips are melted. Remove the pan from the heat.

5. Add the vanilla extract, stirring until the mixture is smooth and glossy. Ask an adult to help you carefully pour the butterscotch into the prepared pan.

6. Immediately microwave the chocolate chips for 30 seconds. Stir the heated chips into a smooth sauce. The chips will not lose their shape until you do this. Quickly stir half-and-half into the melted chocolate so that it will be liquid enough to pour.

7. Drizzle spoonfuls of the melted chocolate in long lines on top of the butterscotch. Next, use the edge of a butter knife to swirl or crisscross the fudge a few times. Don't overdo it, or the two colors will mix together.

8. Chill the fudge until it sets up enough to slice (about 2 to 3 hours). Lift the ends of the parchment paper to remove the fudge from the pan. Peel off the paper, and slice the fudge into 2-inch pieces.

Ingredients

¼ cup semisweet chocolate chips

1 (14 oz) can sweetened condensed milk

1 (11 oz) bag white chocolate chips

1 (11 oz) bag butterscotch chips

1 tsp vanilla extract

3 tsp half-and-half

Tip

You can use metal cookie cutters to cut the fudge into fun shapes instead of squares.

Ingredients

2 flour tortillas

1 Tbsp butter, melted

Colored sugar

Tip

You can't go wrong decorating a magic wand. Try this recipe with cinnamon sugar!

Bibbidi-Bobbidi-Boo Magic Wands

Makes 2 dozen

The phrase "bibbidi-bobbidi-boo" may sound like gibberish, but when Cinderella's fairy godmother says it and waves her wand, all kinds of incredible things start to happen. These sugar-sprinkled wands may just spread a little magic, too.

Directions

1. Heat the oven to 375°F. Line a baking sheet with parchment paper.

2. Use kitchen scissors to cut the tortillas into long ¾-inch-wide strips.

3. Ask an adult to help you at the oven. Arrange the strips on the parchment paper, and bake them for 2 minutes. With a spatula, flip the strips over and bake them for 1 or 2 more minutes.

4. Use a pastry brush to lightly coat each baked wand with melted butter, and then sprinkle on a pinch or two of colored sugar.

Snow White's Apple Dumplings

Makes 4

Snow White would never let one bad experience with an apple keep her from enjoying her favorite dessert-time treat. Whenever she visits the Dwarfs, she makes sure to serve up a batch of her amazing apple dumplings.

Directions

1. Heat the oven to 375°F. Butter an 8- or 9-inch square glass baking pan.

2. To make the dough, whisk together the flour, baking powder, salt, and nutmeg in a mixing bowl. Cut the butter into small pieces, and use your fingertips to pinch them into the flour mixture until the lumps are the size of peas. Stir the milk into the flour mixture.

3. Turn the dough onto a floured surface, and knead it several times so that it holds together. Dust the top of the dough with flour, and then roll it into a 12-inch square.

4. Cut the dough into four equal squares. Place 2 apple quarters and one piece of butter on each square.

5. In a small bowl, mix together the brown sugar and the ¼ teaspoons of cinnamon and nutmeg. Spoon the mixture onto the apples, dividing it equally between the dumplings.

6. To finish each dumpling, moisten the edges of the dough with water. Then, gather the dough corners together on top of the apple pieces and pinch them together. Place the dumplings in the pan, spaced about 1 inch apart.

7. Combine the syrup ingredients together in a small pitcher. Stir well, and pour the syrup into the pan with the dumplings. Ask an adult to help you with the oven. Bake the dumplings for 20 to 25 minutes, until the tops are golden brown and the apples tender.

8. Allow the dumplings to cool for a few minutes. Then spoon some syrup over the top, and serve.

Ingredients

Dough
1½ cups flour
1 tsp baking powder
½ tsp salt
¼ tsp nutmeg
3 Tbsp cold butter
½ cup milk

Filling
2 peeled apples, cored and cut into quarters
1 Tbsp butter, cut into quarters
3 Tbsp brown sugar
¼ tsp cinnamon
¼ tsp nutmeg

Syrup
1 cup hot water
½ cup packed brown sugar
2 Tbsp butter, melted

Tip

Firm apples, like Granny Smiths, Jonathans, or Red Romes, work especially well for this recipe.

1 dozen frosted cupcakes

2 Tbsp extra frosting

24 green gumdrops

12 sour apple gummy ring candies

12 spearmint leaves candies

24 mini chocolate chips

Tip

Instead of mini chocolate chips, you can use candy eyeballs or draw eyes yourself with an edible marker

Sea Turtle Cupcakes

Makes 1 dozen

As a mermaid, Ariel loved to make friends with baby sea turtles. Now that she's a human, she likes to remember her old friends with these adorable cupcakes!

Directions

1. For each cupcake, make a candy turtle shell by cutting a gumdrop in half, horizontally. Use a small dab of frosting to stick the top half of the gumdrop to the center of a gummy ring. Set the shell in the middle of the cupcake top, pressing down slightly to stick it in place.

2. For fins, set a spearmint leaves candy on a cutting board with the rounded side on top. Ask an adult to help you with the knife. Slice the candy in half from top to bottom.

3. Set one of the halves cut side down, and use the tip of a kitchen knife to make a curved cut that slices off the rounded ridge top. Do the same with the other half of the candy. Set the curved ridged pieces in place on the cupcake for the turtle's front flippers, and use the remaining bottom pieces for the back flippers.

4. For the turtle's head, apply a tiny dab of frosting to the back of a mini chocolate chip. Then stick the "eyeball" to the upper-right side of a gumdrop. Attach another mini chocolate chip to the opposite side of the gumdrop.

5. Set the gumdrop head on the cupcake at the front of the shell, gently pressing the very bottom portion into the frosting to stick it in place.

Samson's Carrot Cookies

Makes 2 dozen

Prince Phillip's horse Samson can be stubborn at times, but he never shies away from helping Aurora. To show her appreciation, the princess bakes him a batch of these colorful cookies. Filled with carrots, oats, and apples, they're a real treat for horses—and people, too!

Directions

1. Heat the oven to 375°F. Line a cookie sheet with parchment paper.

2. In a small bowl, whisk together the flour, baking powder, salt, cinnamon, and nutmeg.

3. In a large bowl, stir together the brown sugar and melted butter. Then, beat in the egg with a fork.

4. Stir the flour mixture into the sugar mixture until the batter is smooth. Then stir in the oats, shredded carrot and apple, walnuts, and cranberries.

5. Drop rounded tablespoons of batter onto the cookie sheet, spacing them about ½ inch apart.

6. Ask an adult to help you at the stove. Bake the cookies until they just begin to turn golden brown on top, about 8 minutes. Leave them on the baking sheet for 2 minutes before moving them to a wire rack to cool.

7. Repeat steps 5 and 6 until you've baked all the batter.

Ingredients

1 cup flour

1 tsp baking powder

½ tsp salt

½ tsp cinnamon

½ tsp nutmeg

½ cup brown sugar

¼ cup melted butter

1 egg, lightly beaten

1 cup rolled oats

1 cup shredded carrot

½ cup shredded apple

½ cup chopped walnuts

⅓ cup dried cranberries

Tip

In a pinch, you can use raisins instead of dried cranberries.

Ingredients

2 cups flour

½ tsp baking soda

½ tsp salt

½ tsp nutmeg

½ cup brown sugar

½ cup white sugar

¾ cup (12 Tbsp) butter, softened

1 egg

1 tsp vanilla extract

2 cups semisweet chocolate chips

½ cup chopped walnuts (optional)

Tip

These mini cookies are perfect for dipping in a tall glass of milk!

Chip's Bite-Size Cookies

Makes 8 dozen

When it comes to baking, Chip certainly learned from the best—Mrs. Potts! And just like his savvy mom, Chip knows that teatime isn't complete without some yummy treats.

Directions

1. Heat the oven to 350°F. Line a cookie sheet with parchment paper.

2. In a small bowl, whisk together the flour, baking soda, salt, and nutmeg.

3. In a large bowl, combine the brown and white sugar. Use a wooden spoon to press the butter into the sugar until the mixture is soft and smooth. Stir in the egg and vanilla extract. Then slowly stir in the flour mixture from step 2.

4. Stir the chocolate chips and chopped walnuts (if you're using them) into the dough.

5. Place 12 slightly rounded tablespoons of dough on the cookie sheet, spaced about ½ inch apart. Press down lightly on the center of each spoonful to flatten the dough slightly.

6. Ask an adult to help you with the oven. Bake the cookies until they just begin to turn golden brown on top (about 6 minutes). Remove them from the oven, and leave them on the baking sheet for 2 minutes before moving them to a wire rack to cool.

7. Repeat steps 5 and 6 until you've baked all the dough.

Toasted Oatmeal Ice Cream

Serves 4

Merida's horse, Angus, loves to munch on raw oats. Merida prefers to mix them in ice cream with this tasty cinnamon syrup.

Directions

1. In a small bowl, stir together the maple syrup, canola oil, cinnamon, and salt. Set the mixture aside.

2. Ask an adult to help you at the stove. Heat the oats in a small, nonstick frying pan over low heat. Stir them gently with a wooden spoon until they are lightly toasted (about 3 minutes).

3. Remove the pan from the heat, and pour in the maple syrup mixture. Quickly stir the oats until they are evenly coated and the syrup stops sizzling. Let the oats cool in the pan for a couple of minutes, then spread them on a tray to finish cooling.

4. Take the ice cream out of the freezer and let it thaw for a few minutes. As soon as it's soft enough, spoon it into a small mixing bowl.

5. Use a wooden spoon to stir the cooled toasted oats into the ice cream. Then spoon the ice cream back into the container, and return it to the freezer. When the ice cream has hardened up again, it's ready to serve.

Ingredients

2 tsp maple syrup

¾ tsp canola oil

⅛ tsp cinnamon

Dash of salt

3 Tbsp rolled oats

1 pint vanilla ice cream

Tip

You can stir in other mix-ins, such as chocolate chips, chopped walnuts, or even crushed berries, along with the toasted oats.

Ingredients

Lemon or vanilla pudding

Fresh blueberries
or blackberries

Whipped cream

Tip

For a yummy snack,
you can make this
treat with yogurt
instead of pudding.

Rapunzel's Towering Parfaits

Makes 2

After discovering the world outside her tower, Rapunzel is very happy she left. Still, Rapunzel likes to remember her old home with this tasty treat's towering layers of pudding, fruit, and whipped cream.

Directions

1. Spoon a little pudding into the bottom of each of two parfait glasses. Top the pudding with a layer of fresh berries, followed by a big dollop of whipped cream.

2. Repeat step 1.

3. Add one more layer of pudding.

4. Top each parfait with a small blob of whipped cream garnished with 1 or 2 fresh berries.

Magical Menus

On their own, each of these recipes is a delicious treat, but add a few dishes together, and you get a complete feast! Take a look at some of the Princesses' favorite meals. Then, try creating your own magical menu!

Rapunzel's Head-Start Breakfast

Pascal's Pancakes
16

Frying-Pan
Eggs
24

Sun Punch
104

Merida's Midday Feast

Bull's-Eye Pizza
48

Triple-licious
Fruit Salad
84

Toasted
Oatmeal
Ice Cream
124

Snow White's Winter Warm-Up Lunch

Seven Dwarfs'
Soup
46

Miner's Mini
Muffins
22

White Hot
Chocolate
108

Ariel's Seaside Picnic

Pasta Shell Salad

40

Under the Sea
Sand-Dollar
Crackers

92

Sweet Sea-Foam
Smoothie

106

Belle's Teatime Treats

Tiana's Down-Home Dinner

Bayou Meatloaf
60

Southern
Spoon Bread
76

Confetti Corn
80

Glossary

A

Al dente—an Italian term used to describe pastas or vegetables that are still firm (instead of soft or mushy) when you're done cooking them. Foods prepared al dente are usually more flavorful than foods that cook longer.

B

Baguette—a long, narrow loaf of French bread with a crisp crust

Bake—to cook ingredients in an oven

Baking sheet—a flat metal pan for baking cookies, biscuits, or breads

Beat—to quickly stir an ingredient or batter with a whisk, electric mixer, or spoon until it is smooth and/or fluffy

Blend—to combine two or more ingredients into a smooth mixture

Broccoli slaw—a variation on traditional coleslaw that uses shredded broccoli instead of cabbage

C

Casserole dish—a glass or ceramic dish with a cover used for cooking and serving foods

Celery salt—a flavored salt made with ground celery seeds

Chop—to cut an ingredient into pieces that are roughly the same size

Coconut milk—a creamy liquid made from the grated white insides of a coconut

Cream—to blend ingredients, typically butter and sugar, into a soft and creamy mixture

Crumbled—broken or rubbed into small pieces

D

Dash—a small amount of an ingredient, such as lemon juice or cinnamon, added to a recipe from the container with a quick shake of the wrist

Dice—to cut foods into small cubes (typically ¼ inch wide)

Dill weed—a sweet herb harvested from the flowering tops of dill plants

Drizzle—to slowly pour a thin stream of liquid or a melted ingredient over another food

Dust—to lightly sprinkle a powdery ingredient, such as confectioners' sugar or flour. Rolling pins are often dusted with flour to keep them from sticking to piecrust, cookie dough, or other foods that are rolled out.

E

Extract—a concentrated flavoring made by soaking certain foods, such as vanilla beans, in water and/or other liquids

F

Fillet—a piece of fish or meat from which the bones have been removed

Flake—to break a piece of food, such as cooked fish, into smaller pieces with a fork

Florets—the bushy tops of broccoli or cauliflower stalks

Fold—to gently blend ingredients by using a spatula to cut through the middle of the batter and then flip the left half of the batter over onto the right half. Stiff beaten egg whites are often folded, rather than stirred, into cake and soufflé recipes to keep as much air in the batter as possible.

G

Garbanzo beans—also called chickpeas, these beans are round and tan with a mild nutty flavor

Garnish—to decorate a prepared recipe with an herb, fruit, or other edible ingredient that adds color and/or texture

Grate—to shred foods, such as coconut, carrots, cheese, or chocolate, into bits or flakes by rubbing them against a grater

Ground—when a dry ingredient has been broken up into very small pieces, often with a powder-like texture

H

Hoisin sauce—a sweet Chinese dipping sauce made from mashed soybeans

K

Knead—to repeatedly fold and press together dough until it is smooth and stretchy. Kneading traps air bubbles produced by the yeast, which is what makes the dough rise.

M

Mince—to chop ingredients, such as garlic cloves, gingerroot, or fresh herbs, extra fine. This evenly distributes the flavor in the dish you are cooking.

Glossary (continued)

P

Paprika—a spice made from ground dried bell or chili peppers

Parchment paper—heat-resistant paper used to line a baking sheet so cookies and other foods won't stick to the pan when you bake them

Pat—to gently tap dough with the palm of your hand

Pie shell—unbaked pie dough that is molded into a pie tin, then baked with the pie filling

Pinch—a small amount of a dry ingredient, such as salt or a ground spice, added to a recipe with your fingertips

Pita bread—a flat, round bread made without yeast

Produce—fresh fruits and vegetables

Proof—to test that yeast is still fresh enough to use by dissolving it in a warm liquid (such as water or milk) mixed with a sprinkling of sugar. The yeast should form small bubbles in the liquid if it is still good.

Purée—to blend food until it is completely smooth

R

Rice wine vinegar—a reddish-brown vinegar made from fermented rice wine. Popular in China, this type of vinegar has a much sweeter taste than Western vinegars.

S

Saucepan—a deep pan with a long handle and a cover that is meant for cooking foods on a stovetop

Sauté—to quickly cook food on the stovetop in a lightly oiled pan

Scald—to heat a liquid to just below its boiling point, causing tiny bubbles to form against the pan

Score—to shallowly cut the surface of a food. Meats are often scored in a crisscross pattern to make them tender, while yeast breads and vegetables, such as cucumbers, are scored to decorate them.

Scramble—to stir and/or break food, such as eggs or hamburger, into small bits while it cooks

Seltzer water—water that has been combined with carbon dioxide, making it bubbly

Separate egg whites—to divide egg whites from their yolks. To do this, remove the top half of the eggshell so that both the yolk and white are still in the bottom half. Working over the bowl, slide the yolk from one half of the shell to the other, letting the egg white fall into the bowl underneath. Pour the yolk into a separate bowl.

Sesame oil—a light vegetable oil made from pressed sesame seeds

Shred—to pull or cut an ingredient into many thin strips

Sift—to remove lumps from a dry ingredient, such as flour or confectioners' sugar, by passing it through a mesh strainer or sifter. This makes the ingredient lighter and easier to mix into a dough or batter.

Simmer—to cook food on the stovetop in liquid heated just to the point at which small bubbles rise to the surface

Snip—to use kitchen scissors to cut an ingredient into small pieces

Soften—to warm butter (either by setting it out at room temperature or heating it in a microwave) until it is easy to combine with a mixture

Sprig—a small piece of an herb, usually including the full stem

Steam—to heat food, such as vegetables, in or over a small amount of boiling water so that it is cooked by the rising steam. Other foods that are sometimes steamed include fish, dumplings, and puddings.

Stir-fry—a Chinese stovetop cooking technique in which vegetables and bits of meat are continually stirred while being cooked in hot oil

Strain—to remove the liquid from food by pouring it into a colander, metal sieve, or cheesecloth. The juice or broth passes through the sieve and the solids are retained.

Sweetened condensed milk—milk that has been mixed with sugar and simmered until half or more of the water in it has evaporated and the remaining liquid is thick and creamy

T

To taste—just enough of a certain ingredient, usually salt, to improve the flavor of a recipe

W

Whip—to beat air into an ingredient, such as cream or egg whites, until it is light and fluffy

Whisk—a long-handled kitchen utensil with a series of wire or plastic loops at the end used to rapidly beat eggs, cream, or other liquids

Index

Index (continued)

Food styling by
Edwina Stevenson

Designed by
Tony Fejeran

Special thanks to
**Nancy Inteli, Kelsey Skea,
and Kurt and Anne Schaefer**

Printed in the United States of America

First Edition

10 9 8 7 6

Library of Congress Control Number: 2011943266

FAC-038091-18337

ISBN 978-1-4231-6324-4

Visit www.disneybooks.com